# Our Lady of Perpetual Realness

### & Other Stories

Published by Metatron
www.onmetatron.com
Montreal Québec Canada

Copyright © Cason Sharpe, 2017
All rights reserved
ISBN 978-1-988355-09-2

Publisher and book design | Ashley Opheim
Editor | Jay Ritchie
Cover art | Fraser Wrighte

First edition
First printing

We acknowledge the support of the Canada Council for the Arts, which last year invested $153 million to bring the arts to Canadians throughout the country.

# OUR LADY OF PERPETUAL REALNESS

CASON SHARPE

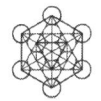

# Our Lady of Perpetual Realness

## & Other Stories

| | |
|---|---|
| MONEY SUCCESS FAME GLAMOUR | 9 |
| CALIFORNIA UNDERWATER | 19 |
| SCAM | 27 |
| DARLING, IF YOU LOVE ME | 41 |
| THE COMING ATTRACTIONS | 51 |
| OUR LADY OF PERPETUAL REALNESS | 61 |

"Everybody wants to leave something behind them, some impression, some mark upon the world. And then you think, you've left a mark upon the world if you just get through it and a few people remember your name. Then you've left a mark. You don't have to bend the whole world. I think it's better to just enjoy it...pay your dues and enjoy it. If you shoot an arrow and it goes real high, hooray for you."
—*Paris Is Burning* (1990)


"There are three important things in life: sex, movies, and my career."
—*Outrageous* (1977)

# MONEY SUCCESS FAME GLAMOUR

BAND SUCKED. I didn't want to be a professional flutist anyway. The other kids in the orchestra didn't even drink. I wanted to be more like Sid. In grade 10, Sid got sent to the office for being drunk in second-period science. He told the vice principal to go fuck herself and then he puked all over her desk. Sid rarely came to class, but he was always roaming the halls with this big rainbow Louis Vuitton handbag dangling from his arm. Beth said it was probably a knock-off.

Sid was the only other gay kid I knew in school. We were both tall, lanky, and brown, but Sid was louder and everyone knew who he was. I wanted to be known like that, even though everyone thought of Sid as this big joke and would imitate the way he swished down the halls behind his back.

I bleached all my jeans and shredded them with a cheese grater to make them more distressed. I started wearing eyeliner to school because it felt like something Sid might do. Beth was like, "OMG, are you trying to be punk now?" Sid started waving at me when we passed in the halls. I waved back. One time between classes he blew me a kiss from the top of a crowded stairwell before disappearing out of view.

Sid never showed up to the third-period English class we had together, but then one day he did. Even Mr. Lyons looked surprised to see him. Sid sat down next to me.

"Hey babe," he said, swinging his big bag onto the table. "What's even going on in this class?" he asked. "I haven't been here in forever."

After school that day I skipped band practice and went over to Beth's. Beth wanted me to help her pick out an outfit. I sat on her bed, under one of those princess canopy things. Beth studied herself in her full-length mirror, alternating between a blue top and a green one. She was going on a date with some 23-year-old she'd met at a club a few weeks before when she borrowed her cousin's ID.

"What do you think about Sid?" I asked her.

"Why?"

"He sat next to me today in English. He called me 'babe.' I don't think he even knows my name."

"He probably wants to fuck you," she said. "Don't go for it. He probably has AIDS or something."

Beth's braces had been off for a year and a half but she still had to wear a retainer at night. She hooked up twice over March Break when she was visiting her cousin, who went to film school in Montreal. She was always handing me unsolicited pieces of advice, especially about guys: who I should and should not hook up with; when I should text them back, if ever.

I'd only ever had sex once, in the summer between grade 10 and 11, with Peter Tony from Oakwood, after a party on St. Clair. We were both very drunk. He had a wooden Ikea bed with drawers underneath and a Biggie poster on his wall. He said he didn't suck dick but I could suck his. It felt like a slippery dim sum roll in my mouth. His pubes smelled like Axe body spray. In the morning his mother made us pancakes and fruit salad, presumably unaware of what her son was doing with his sleepover buddies after dark. When I left his house he told me not to tell anyone what had happened. I saw Peter at parties after that but we never talked. Beth told me he'd said some weird things about black people and he wasn't even that cute so I should just forget about him. She said that I was technically still a virgin because blowjobs didn't really count; it wasn't really like fucking.

We chose the green top. I went home for dinner. Beth went on her date.

Sid started coming to English class more regularly after that.

"I'm trying to get my grades up," he said. He always sat next to me and asked for a pen, or clarification about homework. He told me that he worked at the all-night Rabba on Bay and Charles and that's why he was always late for school and why he sometimes left in the middle of the day, to take a nap. It made it hard to remember homework stuff. "It's all so confusing," he said. "But you seem smart. I'm gonna stick by you and maybe it'll rub off on me."

I started stealing loose cigarettes from my older

sister and smoking them, crushed flat, with Sid every morning outside the school gates. I tried to make sure I was smoking the right way, the way that makes the smoke go down to your lungs and not just swish around in your mouth like hot toothpaste. We talked about trying to quit. We talked about other shit, too. Sid said he was thinking about getting snakebite piercings or maybe a tattoo, but he couldn't decide what he wanted. I told him I was thinking about dyeing my hair blond.

"You should come over sometime," Sid said one morning. "Everyone here sucks, but you're actually kind of cool." I wondered if he saw in me what I saw in him.

Sid lived by himself in an apartment on Church Street, above a Pizza Pizza. I skipped band practice to go over there one day later that week. I wondered why Sid lived alone, or how he could even afford it. He didn't mention his family that much, and when he did, it was cryptic. He said his mom was totally chill and he got his pot from an older half-brother.

His apartment was one open room with a small kitchenette sectioned off in the corner. His futon bed was covered in laundry. Books and DVDs on a shelf, an ashtray, a circular shag rug on the bathroom floor, a Georgia O'Keeffe poster, a plastic lime-green coffee table—it was hard to believe that all of it was Sid's alone.

"Do you think Mr. Lyons is gay?" he asked me. He was lying on his side on the futon, his head propped up on his elbow.

"Maybe," I said, staring out the window that looked out onto Wellesley. I could see men with grey beards walking around in short shorts, rainbow flags draped outside storefronts, a TD Bank.

"Come here," said Sid. He grabbed my hand and pulled me down to the bed so I was lying on top of him. We made out for a while. Two fruit flies boxed overhead.

Sid abruptly pulled away from me and stood up.

"Do you want a cup of tea?" he asked. I felt I had disappointed him in some way. I never learned how to kiss properly. I was a bit taller than Sid, which made it difficult to get comfortable. My height was an issue with Peter too; my legs had dangled off the edge of his Ikea bed. Maybe it was my lips or my tongue, too wet or too dry, too little or too much of something.

"Yeah, sure," I said. He put on the water for tea, lit a cigarette, and sat next to me on the futon.

"School is really some bullshit, eh?" he said. I didn't know if he wanted an answer, so I nodded. "I'm going to move to L.A. to be a porn star." He said he'd been fooling around with a video camera he'd bought for cheap at a pawn shop in Chinatown. He already had his porn alias picked out: Jack Spooner. "What are you going to do?" he asked me.

"I don't know. Probably university or something." The kettle whistled and we drank tea. I asked him why he wanted to be a porn star.

"I guess I just like it when everybody's looking at me. And paying attention." He asked me if I understood what he meant. I mentioned something about my flute solo in the winter concert. Sid got up and looked out the window like I wasn't even there. Then he turned to me and said he had to get ready for work. Sid bought his own cigarettes and lived in his own apartment and was going to L.A. to be naked all the time. I felt super dumb about the whole thing. I had to get home for dinner anyway. He said he had Saturday off, so I should come over again. I didn't know whether to kiss him goodbye or shake his hand so I just left.

I skipped band practice again after school the next day to go over to Beth's. I sat on her bed with the princess canopy thing and she stood in front of the full-length mirror, debating blue top or green top. I figured that if I missed enough rehearsals they'd eventually kick me out of band.

"So what, are you guys like dating now?" Beth asked me when I told her what had happened at Sid's.

"No, I don't think so. I think we're just like, friends." I didn't tell her that we had plans to hang out on Saturday.

Beth was going to meet up with the 23-year-old for drinks on Queen West. "It's so nice to hang out with older people," she said. "You know one of his friends DJs at Wrongbar like every night?" She said older guys were better at sex than younger ones, but she didn't know if that was true for gay guys. Beth knew I didn't have a fake ID and she was always meeting these new people at bars. It was like she was purposely leaving me out so she could tell me about it later and gloat. This time she chose the blue top.

On Saturday I went back over to Sid's. He said he was in a bad mood. He spoke really quickly and chain-smoked. He said that school was such bullshit, they were trying to suspend him for missing too many classes or something, but he hadn't even been skipping that much lately and now his mom was pissed at him. It was that vice principal, that *bitch*, she didn't like him because one time he yelled at her when he got sent to the office. I didn't tell him the version that I'd heard. Work sucked and he was going to quit soon because his boss was being a total asshole. He'd caught Sid stealing a bag of Cheetos and a copy of *Us Weekly* and said he was going to take it out of Sid's paycheque. Sid had been trying to save up for L.A. but all his money went to smokes and food and rent that he split with his mom's boyfriend fifty-fifty. He sat down next to me on the futon.

"Hey," he said. "Would you tutor me, in English or whatever? You're really smart and I need to get my grades up."

"I'm not that smart," I said.

"Whatever," he said. "I just need like a C." I agreed to tutor him once a week. He offered to pay me, but I told him not to worry about it. I was happy to help.

Sid smiled. He said I was cute. I thought he was cute too. We made out. He kept making little noises from the back of his throat, and when I opened my eyes for a second I saw him sort of grinning, like I had told a really funny joke. He took his shirt off and his thinness became an unavoidable fact, shadows tracing ribs and clavicle across his dark chest.

Sid turned away from me and dug around his piles of clothes until he unearthed the video camera.

"We should film this," he said. "The light is perfect right now." I thought he was joking, but he pulled a tripod out of his closet and started to set it up. "We could probably make money off of it, if we put it on the internet or whatever."

"Yeah," I said. "Let's do it."

We moved the coffee table aside and pushed the futon right up against the windowed wall. Sid adjusted the height of the tripod and the angle of the camera, placing them at the foot of the bed before he climbed back into it. He put his arm around me and spoke directly into the camera.

"I'm Jack Spooner, and me and this sexy guy right here..." he rubbed a few quick circles across my chest with his palm, "we're going to have some fun for you guys today." Sid kissed me on the cheek. "Wave to our fans," he instructed. I looked directly into the camera and waved.

We started kissing again. When Sid took off my shirt my skin goose-pimpled. We wriggled out of our tight jeans, turning them inside-out as we slid them off along with our underwear. Sid sat on the edge of the futon and I knelt before him. He was framed by the window, backlit by the streaming sun. When I took his cock into my mouth he took a deep breath in, expanding his exposed ribcage and sending it upward to create a deep cavern in the middle of his torso. He said it felt good, really really good.

My phone started ringing. I stood up and grabbed it out of the pocket of my discarded jeans. It was Beth.

"Can you talk?" she said. Her voice sounded distressed and unsure. Un-Beth-like.

"I'm kind of in the middle of something," I said.

"You're with Sid, aren't you?" The word "*Sid*" bit my

ear like a rabid dog. I excused myself to the bathroom. "He broke up with me, just so you know." I could tell she had been crying. Her words came out between hiccups and globs of snot. The 23-year-old was getting back together with his ex, who studied Digital Media at OCAD and had a bunch of trashy tattoos. "And she's not even from Toronto," Beth said. "She's from Oakville or something, and she wears frumpy skirts that make her ass look big." The 23-year-old had just shrugged and said she was a cool kid but it wasn't like they were really dating anyway. He was a fucking bastard and she was a cunt and Beth wished them a long happy life together.

Poor Beth. Beth who brought me flat ginger ale in bed when I was sick, who sat front-row during the winter concert and cheered the loudest during my flute solo. I pictured her in the green top and then again in the blue top, and both times she looked too young to trick a bouncer. I felt strangely vindicated by the image, and then ashamed by how pleased it had made me, which left me with a frustrating sense of futility. Bittersweet, like the way weekends can be.

"I love you," I said. I told her that I had to go, but I'd come over later with ice cream. Beth said yeah, sounds good, like she wanted to believe me but didn't. I hung up the phone and stepped out of the bathroom.

Sid was lying naked on the futon with the video camera in his hands, watching the footage we'd just shot. I heard his introduction, slightly garbled in the playback, the barely audible pop of a kiss, and the skittering of loose change across cold linoleum. Sid's eyes watched the camera screen with a dissatisfied focus, like a kid whose Lego tower didn't look quite like the one on the box. He was my image in reverse, the exact opposite and the exact same, but we'd been standing too close to each other for me to see it until just then. I wondered if L.A. was just a fantasy, one that got blurrier the harder you tried to find it. The sun was starting to sink outside the window. It lit up what it could and the rest was left in shadows. Sid, his eyes still fixed on the camera, said, "Hey, can you grow a beard?"

# CALIFORNIA UNDERWATER

I WORK at a big movie theatre downtown where everyone is a teenager except for me. At first it was fun but now I just feel pathetic and creepy. It was supposed to be a temporary thing—I had just finished school and had no money and needed a job immediately, etc.—but then somehow it became a not-temporary thing. Somehow it has been over a year. I work six days a week and sometimes doubles, from the first screening straight through to the last. I'm not even the manager. Kevin is the manager and also a freshman at U of T.

† 

Teresa and some of the other girls who work at the theatre ask me to pick up alcohol for them one evening. They want to let loose because it's summer vacation but they keep getting carded and the guy at the LCBO won't accept Teresa's ID, even though she borrowed it from her older sister. I agree, and they hand me a wad of bills and a list of their requests written on the back of a discarded ticket stub: a couple coolers and few mickeys of Smirnoff. In the liquor store the cashier looks disapprovingly at my purchases, which makes me feel stupid. I know the cashier probably thinks I'm some hoodlum who's off to drink shitty vodka and smoke blunts with his boys in a basement somewhere, but I don't have the energy to disprove her assumptions by making conversation so I just pay for the stuff and get the fuck out. When I bring the alcohol back to the girls, they're so excited and grateful that I feel pretty pleased with myself. I'm ashamed by how earnestly I want to impress a group of 17-year-olds, just like the closet case I was back in high school.

The next day Kevin asks to speak with me privately. Earlier that morning someone found one of the storage rooms littered with empty liquor bottles, cigarette butts, and a slick pile of puke. Kevin gives me a lecture about buying alcohol for minors.

"Do whatever you want on your own time," he says. "But keep it out of the theatre." Kevin is a twerp, but also what the fuck Teresa? I direct my embarrassment and anger nowhere in particular so it spills out everywhere, untamed and clumsy. I hand back the wrong change a couple of times and I snap at a customer when they ask me for directions to the bathroom.

†

After work I meet up with Kelly at a bar on Dundas. Kelly just got back from L.A., where he recently had a show. I'm happy for him, but he's already selling out. He's cuffed his

Levi's. He wears a worn baseball cap and white T-shirt like he's a tradesman and not a figurative oil painter dabbling in video work whose parents happen to be two of the most celebrated architects in the city. I ask him how he liked L.A.

"It was trippy," he says. There's a water shortage throughout California but rich people and celebrities still power-wash their sidewalks. He met a Belgian curator who said he couldn't wait for the tsunami to come and submerge the entire state underwater. Only the worthy will survive. True artists will be granted gills to attend their aquatic openings. Kelly asks me how my practice is going.

"What practice?" I say, laughing. I haven't so much as touched a paintbrush in over six months. We chat about people from art school—this person has a residency, and that person got a write-up in *Canadian Art*, and so-and-so insulted whoever-the-fuck on Instagram. Art school was such a waste of time and money, in retrospect. From the first day it was clear who would eventually make a career out of it and who wouldn't. I could've schmoozed with my professors more the way Kelly did. I could've tried to ride the diversity quotas, maybe gotten my paintings in a group show or two, but there's basically a waiting list to be the next Hot Black Artist at this point. I don't even know if I give a shit about art anymore. The whole thing just seems kind of stupid. When everything is underwater none of this will matter. Buoyed by this thought plus a few more beers, I'm peaceful enough that when I get home I fall easily into bed and sleep like a baby.

†

The next day at work, Teresa and Eric get into this massive fight in front of everyone in the theatre, including all of the customers. It starts off small and gets louder and louder until everyone is frozen watching them go at it behind the concession stand. Eric calls Teresa a stupid bitch.

Teresa says, "So what, you're just some dumb faggot." Then she dumps a cup full of Coke on his head. Someone has called Kevin in at this point. He breaks the two apart and apologizes to the customers. Everyone is buzzing from the drama. *Who started it? She's so angry all the time. Eric is such a kiss-ass.* I know that this is going to lead to some big team meeting about appropriate work behaviour and giving the customer the experience they paid for and blah blah blah.

I sneak outside for a cigarette break. Teresa is sitting on the front steps leading up to the theatre having a smoke. She waves.

"Hey," I say.

"Hey," she says. "Kevin sent me home for the day." I sit down next to her. We smoke in silence for a little while, staring at the street in front of us.

"Look," she says. "I'm sorry. I didn't mean—like, I'm not homophobic or whatever." I laugh.

"Don't worry about it," I say. "No big deal."

"Sometimes I just get so angry," she says. "And I don't know what to do so I end up saying all this stupid shit."

"I totally get it," I say. I do.

"He sucks. You know he's the one that ratted us out

the other night, in the storage room? Kevin put me on probation. I'm probably going to get fired now."

"Yeah, fuck Eric. I always thought he was a little prick."

"I don't want to get fired," she says. "I like it here. And I need the money."

"If Kevin fires you, I'll quit in protest." Teresa smiles. We talk about life for a bit. Teresa wants to go to school in Montreal after she graduates next year, maybe study psychology at McGill. Or maybe she'll stay here and get a job at Aritzia. Her sister Carmen works there and they might be hiring soon. I tell her about Kelly and the Belgian curator and California underwater.

"You really think that'll happen?" she asks.

"I don't know," I say. "Maybe."

†

The following evening I meet Teresa and Carmen in Christie Pits to drink a few beers in the crater of the park. Carmen is the same age as me. I can tell that at first she's like, *What the fuck, why are you hanging out with my younger sister?* I act really swishy until she figures out that I'm not trying to hit on Teresa and then she softens. Turns out she knows Kelly and a bunch of other people I know, but that's not surprising. Everyone who grew up downtown in my age bracket kind of knows each other.

"So Kelly's like some big artist now?" Carmen asks. "I remember in high school he always used to tag shit with my ex-boyfriend."

"I guess so," I say. "He just had a show in L.A."

"Mikey says that California's gonna be underwater any day now," says Teresa. Carmen glances at me sidelong.

"There's supposed to be this big tsunami coming on the West Coast," I say. "Like the one that happened in Japan in 2011 or whatever, but on the other side of the Pacific. They say it'll hit the Alaskan coast and then go all the way down B.C. to California. It's been predicted for years now but it still hasn't come."

"Shit," says Carmen. "Florida's supposed to be fucked too, 'cause of rising sea levels and shit."

We drink more beer and Carmen rolls a joint. We talk about normal, boring stuff: movies we like, which TV shows we're watching, how irritating our coworkers and managers can be. Carmen is the manager at Aritzia, so she tells us about it from the other side. The more we talk the more I realize I haven't been around people my own age who aren't pretentious art-school kids or people from my high school in a really long time. I make a mental note to ask Carmen for her number at the end of the evening. When I stand up to go pee in the bushes, a head rush tells me that I am very, very fucked up.

When I get back from peeing, Teresa's like, "Hey, do you want to go swimming?"

†

Carmen and Teresa book it right the fuck over the chain-link fence, toss their clothes on the deck, and cannonball into the water. Too headstrong and embarrassed to ask for a boost, I watch the two of them splash around while I shimmy and grunt my way up the fence. When I finally get to the other side, I trip on a pant leg while trying to slip it off. I fall into the water as though into a hug, laughing.

"This is so chill!" I say once my head has bobbed to the surface. "Isn't this so chill?" Carmen and Teresa laugh. "It really is so chill, though!"

Teresa goes down the waterslide. She lands with a tremendous splash. I go under again and swim around with my eyes open. Everything is wiggly greens and whites.

Maybe I should go to L.A. Maybe the tsunami won't be so bad. Maybe I would be granted gills. They'll need movie theatres underwater, right? And what good will painting be, after we're all submerged? Every canvas will be wiped clean anyway. The only skill that will matter is how you stay afloat.

I pull myself out of the water. Carmen's like, "Hey, is everything cool?"

I'm like, "Yeah, yeah. I'm gonna call Kelly. Kelly should come! I'm gonna call Kelly." Then I grab my phone out of my jeans pocket and call Kelly.

†

I wake up the next morning two-and-a-half hours late for work. My head is throbbing and everything feels like shit. I have five missed calls: one from the National Student Loan Centre, one from Teresa, two from Kevin, one from Kelly. They can wait 'til later. They can wait 'til never. Until after we're all underwater. I walk to the Loblaws down the street from my apartment to get Advil and orange juice. I wander through the aisles for what feels like forever, like a fish paddling laps in its bowl.

# SCAM

> Da Mayor: Doctor...
> Mookie: C'mon, what. What?
> Da Mayor: Always do the right thing.
> Mookie: That's it?
> Da Mayor: That's it.
> Mookie: I got it, I'm gone.
> —*Do the Right Thing* (1989)

## MONDAY

### 9:15 a.m. — A Smart Thing in a Dumb World

SEAN CALLS me into his office.

"Your sales are low," he says. He's sitting in an ergonomic chair with a high back. I'm facing him in a small plastic chair with legs so low I have to pull my knees into my chest like an overgrown kindergartener. There's a big wooden desk in between us. I can't tell if the small potted fern at the edge of the desk is wilting or just starting to grow.

"You had a lot of promise at first, but recently you haven't been delivering," says Sean. "If you have the lowest sales at the end of the week, I'll have to let you go."

I'm like, *Fuck you, Sean*, but I just nod because I need the job and when Sean smiles I want him to like me.

"You've got to be more of a shark," he says. He gets up and stands in front of me, his hips at eye level. He puts a hand on my shoulder. "I know you have it in you," he says.

Sean is a shark. Sean is our boss. Sean—the boss, the shark—wears a fitted cap and a diamond stud in his ear. He has freckles and a big frame like a linebacker. Sometimes his sports jersey rides up his back when he bends over and you can see the elastic waistband of his boxer shorts peeking out from under his low-rise jeans. Every morning he stands on a chair and gives a speech to the rows of cubicles that stretch across the office. He'll say cheesy shit like, "Success is where preparation and opportunity meet!"

Sean says that the world is divided into sharks and non-sharks. The shark is a smart thing in a dumb world. The non-shark is everyone else. Everyone else is dumb. This is what Sean tells us. Non-sharks think that they're sharks, but they're not. They don't know what they are. This is how you make the sale. Convince the customer he's a shark and he'll buy.

## 9:30 a.m. — Totally Not a Shark

Back in my cubicle. Half-doing a newspaper sudoku. No calls yet from the autodialer.

Our job is to sell magazine subscriptions at an inflated price over the phone. This is the deal: If a customer commits to a three-year subscription to five magazines at a total cost of $1,500, we'll give them an all-expenses paid trip to a tropical destination of their choice. What we don't tell the customers is that we only offer subscriptions to a limited selection of second- and third-rate magazines (*Reader's Digest*, for instance, and some teen pop magazines à la *Tiger Beat*) and the tropical vacation is actually a timeshare pitch. The office is in the Old Port. Men in horse-drawn carriages wait outside our building to cart around tourists for 50 bucks a ride. Sean drives a white Escalade and pays us $10.75 an hour.

In the cubicle to my right is Ramon, who has a lazy eye and deals weed on the side. In the cubicle directly facing mine is Claire, who has a tattoo of a heart on her throat and lives with her boyfriend in Parc Ex. Claire and Ramon are both sharks. Sabrina is in the cubicle to my left. She's originally from B.C. and goes to Concordia for Philosophy with a minor in Sustainability Studies. She has a jagged haircut and dresses all punk and lives in St. Henri. When I tell her that I also live in St. Henri she's like, "Really?" because I'm not covered in patches or whatever. I want to be like, *Look, I know you probably have some rich parents in Vancouver so don't act like I'm this big evil gentrifier.*

Sometimes Sabrina and I take the metro home together after work and complain about how shitty everything is. Sabrina's always like, "This place is so corrupt! Sean is just like, *Sell sell sell*, and these poor people, they don't even know they're being ripped off. I can't believe how fucked up it is. Capitalism at its finest."

I like Sabrina; we get along fine, but even I can tell that she's totally not a shark.

## 10:15 a.m. — Fridays Are Mostly Just Really Sad (Still Monday)

To get us hyped up to take calls, Sean explains the bonus/commission system again. Every Friday, Sean tallies up all of our sales for the week and whoever has the most sales gets a $150 bonus added to their next paycheque. Nidia is always the top seller. Apparently she used to work at the bank fraud helpline at CIBC, so she knows how to sound professional over the phone when dealing with people's credit card information. Once she sold a subscription to *Men's Health* to a blind guy.

"But even if you don't get the bonus, there's still commission," says Sean. "Free money in your pocket. If you make one to two sales per day every day this week, you get an extra three dollars per sale. If you make three to four sales per day every day this week, you get an extra six dollars per sale…"

All of that information is irrelevant, because nobody ever makes commission anyway. You're lucky if you get one sale a day. Whoever has the lowest number of sales by the end of the week gets fired. Fridays at the office are mostly just really sad.

# TUESDAY

### 9:15 a.m. — I Didn't Know You Went to McGill

Sean makes me pull up a chair next to Nidia in her cubicle and listen to her calls for the morning. Nidia and all the other top sellers sit in a row of cubicles next to Sean's office. This row is known as Shooter Alley. A shooter is like a shark but better, like a next-level shark.

"It's just about telling people what they want to hear," says Nidia. "And finding a point of connection. Like the other day, I had this lady on the phone from Westmount, right? She was totally resistant, just an all-around bitch. Then I asked her about her family. She said she had a son who was doing his Master's at McGill. I told her that I also went to McGill, what was his name? When she told me I was like, *Oh yeah, I totally think I've heard that name before, he's doing some really interesting research I hear…*"

"I didn't know you went to McGill," I say.

"I don't," says Nidia. "The point is, I made the sale."

For the second half of the morning, I'm allowed to return to my cubicle to practice the new skills I have learned.

### 2:30 p.m. — On the Phone with My Mother

"Yeah, it's OK I guess. I'm not that great at it. I think they'll fire me soon."

"I mean, yeah, there's definitely something sketchy going on. My boss drives an Escalade. Like, how can you make that much money off magazine subscriptions, and we're only calling the most random people. Who even has a landline anymore?"

"Yeah, I think it's a front, probably. I don't think it's drugs, like maybe something with the mob or the internet?"

"Yeah, I'm OK for money right now. How about you?"

## 12:47 p.m. — Lunch Break

I buy a dime bag of weed off Ramon.

"This is really good shit," he says, but I know that's just a thing that dealers say. I wouldn't know the difference. I don't smoke a lot, but I figure it'll give me something fun to look forward to after work.

"How much?" I ask.

"Don't worry about it," says Ramon. He gives me a sad kind of smile.

## 6:00 p.m. — Stoned

I start taking apart my room, rearranging furniture, taking down framed pictures and posters and putting them back on the wall in new positions. I take horrible before and after photos, too much flash. I wonder how much it all cost me cumulatively over the years: the bed, the dresser, the nightstand, etc.

I put on my pyjamas, eat a can of tuna, watch an episode of *Will & Grace* in bed. When the episode is finished I'm too lazy to load another one. I stare at the ceiling. I think about Sean driving around in his white Escalade.

## WEDNESDAY

### 12:30 p.m. — Eat or Be Eaten

I ask Nidia about the whole CIBC bank fraud thing.

"That seems like a pretty sweet gig," I say. "Why would you give that up to come work here?"

She's like, "Yeah, it was fine, but I had to deal with all these idiots. Like people who would use the ATM at sketchy dive bars or give their credit card number to some online scam, like who the fuck does that? And the amount of people who 'lose' their debit card is crazy. I've been fucked up before but I've never just completely lost my debit card. Even when I'm smashed I always know where my wallet is. Like don't you understand the value of a dollar? There were just too many stupid people at CIBC and I was through with helping the helpless. They're going to get screwed anyway, so you might as well make a buck off it. Eat or be eaten, you know?"

### 5:30 p.m. — Good Versus Evil Thing

Sabrina and I decide to go see a movie. On the metro to the theatre I tell her about what Nidia told me.

"OMG," she says, "Eat or be eaten? That's such bullshit. She's always flirting with Sean. It's so pathetic."

"Yeah," I say, "totally." But I do find it annoying when people get all upset after doing careless things like randomly losing their debit cards.

We get off the metro at Atwater and go to the Cineplex Forum. It used to be the big hockey arena in the '70s or whatever and now it's a movie theatre. Giant Montreal Canadiens flags are draped from the ceiling and a section of the original bleachers still sits in the atrium, a few of the seats filled with these creepy plaster mannequins wearing blue and red jerseys.

It's summer so nothing much is playing, just big-budget blockbuster junk. I want to go to the action-adventure one, it's the third part of a franchise and I've seen the first two.

"Isn't that a kids' movie?" says Sabrina.

"I love kids' movies," I say. Sabrina is skeptical but she agrees because Ezra Miller is in it.

The movie is OK. It's a classic good-versus-evil thing. Evil is wreaking havoc and good can't decide upon the best course of action, which causes even more pandemonium, and then of course some of the good people turn out to be secretly evil and some of the evil people turn out to be secretly good. The hero's sidekick gets a few funny gags and one-liners. The whole thing lasts about an hour and forty-five minutes, including the previews.

After the movie, Sabrina and I walk down the big hill on Atwater to go back to St. Henri. We smoke cigarettes and split the last of Sabrina's popcorn, which she hadn't finished in the theatre.

"I can't believe you like that stuff," she says. "It was so cheesy."

"The other two were better," I say. "But this one wasn't bad."

"It was so heavy-handed!" says Sabrina.

"Of course it was heavy-handed," I say. "It's a kids' movie!" Sabrina laughs.

"For a second I forgot about work tomorrow," she says. "Sean says if I don't make a sale by the end of the week I'm fired."

"Same."

It's a warm night out, but there's a bit of a breeze.

# THURSDAY

### 9:03 a.m. — Blowjob Gesture

I walk into the office and there's no chair at my cubicle. Sean has taken it away. He's taken a bunch of them away. Only Nidia is allowed to sit.

"She's been carrying the rest of you for too long," says Sean. Ramon does a blowjob gesture by pressing his tongue against his cheek and jerking a loose fist in front of his mouth.

"When you make a sale, you can have your seat back," says Sean. Sabrina looks at me and rolls her eyes. I put two fingers to my temple and pretend to fire them like a gun.

### 12:30 p.m. — A Big White Horse and Carriage

Still haven't made a sale yet. Neither has Sabrina.

"This is such bullshit," she says. I nod.

We get pulled pork sandwiches on Kaiser buns from this little dep down the street from the office. We eat them sitting outside on the curb. My feet are killing me.

"I have to make a sale or I'm fucked for rent," says Sabrina.

"Same." A big white horse pulling a carriage full of tourists trots past us.

"Take me with you!" Sabrina screams after it. It's like the funniest thing she's ever said.

"Nidia was right," I say. "It is eat or be eaten. You're either a crook or you're fired."

"This is such bullshit," Sabrina says again. She stands up. "You coming?"

"Nah," I say. "I'm gonna stay here and finish my sandwich. I'll see you up there." Sabrina nods and walks back to the office.

What a depressing summer. I haven't been to the pool, not even once. Broke as shit, too. I want a good job. I want to work with children, or maybe old people. I want a job that can pay the rent and a job that I can call my mom about and feel proud. I see Sean's Escalade parked across the street. If I get fired I'll egg it or write something on the hood in permanent marker, just to be like, *Fuck you*. I can feel my heart getting smaller. Maybe I should quit before they can fire me. My phone starts ringing in the pocket of my jeans.

## 12:47 p.m. — On the Phone With God/The Universe/A Higher Power, etc.

"If you're worried about the morality of your current position, think about all the underpaid writers who pen all the articles in those shitty magazines you make people subscribe to, think about the printers and the graphic designers, think about the people who make ink."

"Think about all the flight attendants who will have to get all your customers safely on and off the plane heading towards the tropical vacation you promised them, and think about all the employees at the timeshare resort who will be forced to sell your customers yet another thing they do not want. Think about the Seans that all of these people have to encounter breathing down their necks every day. There are a limitless supply of Seans in this world. Each Sean has their own Sean."

"There may not be any magazines or tropical destinations at all. The whole operation could be as big of a scam as you suspect, possibly bigger. For now, everything sucks and complicity in this system isn't exactly chill, but it's all so much larger than you, and your hands are tied by a certain limited range of meaningful options. If you bail just because you feel like bailing, you'll end up taking a position out of desperation at another company with a similar degree of moral bankruptcy that just manifests itself in some other way. The thing about sharks is that they don't actually live in the deepest parts of the ocean and are therefore unable to perceive the true scope of their ecosystem."

"The best course of action for you now is to keep a low profile. Do the bare minimum to avoid getting fired while you actively look for something else but don't stress out about it too much and don't rely on Craigslist. If/when a new opportunity presents itself in which you can fuck over the smallest amount of people possible and still pay your rent, that's when you should quit."

### 1:13 p.m. — Wouldn't It Be Nice?

A couple of people have earned their seats back after lunch. I start to get nervous. My voice becomes dry and strained. I have trouble focusing on whatever the voices are saying on the other end of the line. I drop two calls back to back. Sean passes by my cubicle.

"Make the next call a sale," he says. "You need it."

I take a deep breath. My next call is with a middle-aged woman in Grand Rapids, Michigan. I deliver the introductory spiel on autopilot while in my head I think about magazines aimed towards working- and middle-class women: *Better Homes and Gardens*, *Good Housekeeping*, *Vanity Fair*. I can feel Sean standing behind me, his arms crossed, watching. I look over at Sabrina, standing in the cubicle next to mine. She's in the middle of a call. Her voice sounds perky but her eyes look like she's about to cry, or maybe punch somebody in the face.

The woman on the phone is interested but can she think about it and give us a call back? I almost blurt out *NO!* but regain composure. Convincing someone to buy is like trying to lure a small animal. You have to tread carefully. No sudden movements. If a customer hears desperation in your voice it'll drive them away. Selling stuff over the phone is all about how you pitch your voice.

For younger women, go slightly higher and more femme, give them that *Yass queen!* gay boy fantasy they trust with dating advice and clothes. For men (age irrelevant), pitch in a lower, more serious tone, like you're in a corporate business meeting. For older women, use soft tones, like you're their favourite grandchild, and don't use *ma'am* because it can sound condescending or sleazy. I am very aware of trying to keep my voice "neutral," which means suppressing any auditory hints of Blackness. I've noticed a lot of people doing it. Even Nidia hides her accent when she's on the phone. These are the things I have learned.

I gently tell the woman that the magazine and vacation package is a limited-time offer but if she's ever dissatisfied with her subscription she can give us a call and we'll gladly cancel it and give her a refund. I can hear Sabrina next to me. She sounds agitated, the pitch of her voice wavering. I feel for Sabrina, but it's also frustrating to listen to her. She doesn't even have to change her voice on the phone and she still can't make a sale.

"I'm still not sure," says the woman from Grand Rapids. I ask her if she has any vacation plans. She says no, she hasn't been able to travel much since her husband got laid off a few years back. I watch Sabrina take off her headset and let it drop to the floor. She runs a hand through her hair. Exhales.

"Wouldn't it be nice to get away?" I ask. "A free vacation, just you and your husband lying on a beach..." I keep my tone even and calm. "Maybe a margarita or two..." I add with a laugh.

We try two different credit cards that both get declined

before the pre-authorized payment finally goes through on an old Amex the woman didn't even know she still had. I make the sale.

"Good job," says Sean, handing me a chair. "But we don't offer refunds. They can cancel their subscription, but they still have to pay." When I sit down, my hands are shaky. I look over to Sabrina's cubicle, but nobody's there. Sean puts a hand on my shoulder. "I knew you were a shark," he says.

# DARLING, IF YOU LOVE ME

SWEETHEART ARRANGES to meet The Man in the passenger pickup area of a subway station at the end of the line. Sweetheart is worried that the passenger pickup area will be busy but when he gets there it's just an empty parking lot. There's a Pizza Pizza, a gas station, and a few cars on the four-lane road that turns onto the highway. Nothing else. Blue skies and a couple of cartoon clouds. Sweetheart lights a cigarette and waits.

It's an afternoon in late August but still as hot as July. Sweetheart is in his skimpiest outfit, a thin tank top and a pair of cut-offs that ride up his thighs. His hairy chicken legs dark brown from all the sun. Sweetheart hopes The Man thinks he looks cute, even though he knows it doesn't matter.

Sweetheart has the day off. He's been getting fewer shifts at the video store recently. No one is renting DVDs anymore. The only thing that keeps the place afloat is the porn section, located behind a beaded curtain in a room double the size of the rest of the store. The only customers are a handful of old men who don't know how to use the internet. They rent the same movies week after week, with titles you'd expect: *Young & Busty xXx*, *College Co-ed Fuck Fest*, *Brazilian Bareback 4*.

The manager of the video store is batshit crazy. He keeps throwing these big temper tantrums because business isn't going well. He fired two employees last month for no apparent reason. Miranda quit a few weeks ago because he wouldn't do anything about the old Portuguese man who kept making passes at her. Miranda keeps being like, "Sweetheart, man, you gotta get out of there. That place is fucked." But where is Sweetheart going to find another job? He doesn't have many skills. He crushes his cigarette butt into the pavement with the edge of his heel. Besides, it's not the worst place to work. The old men don't make passes at him, but sometimes he has to ask them not to jack off in the store.

A grey minivan pulls into the passenger pickup area. Sweetheart knows it's The Man because The Man told him he'd be driving a grey minivan via a text exchange earlier that morning. The Man lowers the window and motions for Sweetheart to get in. The grey minivan slows down as it passes but doesn't stop.

†

The first time The Man came into the video store, Sweetheart and Miranda were standing behind the counter. It must've been a few months ago. Sweetheart remembers because the store doesn't see new customers very often.

"Look at this creep," Miranda said.

"Yeah," said Sweetheart, although he didn't find The Man as gross as the usual clientele. The Man wore wireframe glasses and a grey suit that swelled under the mass of his belly. His face looked bloated and warm in a way that reminded Sweetheart of Santa Claus. He had a salt-and-pepper beard, and his thinning hair was slicked back with gel. Sweetheart watched The Man disappear behind the beaded curtain. He didn't find him attractive, but he wasn't exactly unattractive either.

The Man came out of the porn section a few minutes later and walked up to the cash with a DVD in hand.

"Do you have a membership?" Sweetheart asked. He didn't. Sweetheart got The Man a membership card and signed out his rental for him. His copy of *Bulging Black Cocks* was due in one week.

The Man returned to the video store the following week to renew his copy of *Bulging Black Cocks*. He returned the week after that, and then again the week after that. He never browsed any of the other DVDs. He just kept renting the same old porno over and over again.

The Man would chat with Sweetheart as he renewed his rental. Through these interactions, Sweetheart learned that The Man lived in the suburbs but commuted into the city every day for his job at an insurance agency downtown. He liked Toronto, but it was too noisy. Not a good place to raise kids. One day, Sweetheart learned that The Man had two kids of his own at home: a boy, 11, and a girl, 16. The boy was well-behaved but the girl, she was always up to no good.

"You probably know what that's like," The Man said. "A good-looking boy like yourself. You must get into all kinds of trouble." Sweetheart smiled. Couldn't help it.

"Maybe," he said.

"Where are you from?" asked The Man.

"Toronto," Sweetheart said.

"No," said The Man. "I mean, what's your background?"

"I'm mixed," he said. "Like, my dad, he was black or whatever."

"I thought so," said The Man. Sweetheart handed the DVD over to him.

"It's due back here in a week."

†

There is no traffic on the highway. Sweetheart sits next to The Man in the passenger seat. He stares out the window. They're driving through that space between what's inside of a city and what's outside of it. There are a few buildings that look like corporate headquarters. A strip mall. The back of a subdivision. Some trees. A patch of grass.

"Can I turn on the radio?" Sweetheart asks.

"I prefer silence," The Man says. He puts a hand on Sweetheart's thigh. Inside the grey minivan it is very clean.

†

The grey minivan pulls up to a roadside motel.

"Wait here," says The Man. He turns off the car and steps out onto the gravel parking lot, slams the door. Sweetheart watches The Man walk towards the motel and then disappear inside it. Facing forward in the passenger seat, Sweetheart can only see the ground floor of the motel's concrete facade: a main entrance on the far right, and then four pink doors lined up in a row, each with a window drawn shut by floral-print curtains. He can't see the highway, but he can feel it surrounding him, the occasional faint hiss of a car driving by.

Sweetheart scrolls through his phone. Miranda posted a picture of herself at the beach on Instagram. Maybe he should call the whole thing off. Tell The Man to forget the motel and drive him back to the subway. He still has time to meet up with Miranda at the beach. It's early in the afternoon; plenty of hours of daylight left to go. But how much is a ticket to take the ferry across to the island? And once he's there he's going to want a beer, and probably dinner from the snack bar they have over there too, and rent is due in two days.

Sweetheart sees The Man re-emerge from the inside of the motel. Sweetheart watches The Man get bigger and bigger as he approaches the grey minivan. The Man opens the passenger-side door and gestures with his fingers for Sweetheart to step out of the car, like the way you would beckon a bird.

†

They're in motel suite number three. The Man unlocks

the pink door and Sweetheart steps inside. There's grey wall-to-wall carpeting, a wooden dresser with a TV on top, and a queen-size bed with floral-print sheets to match the curtains. The curtains are so thick that barely any light can make it in. From inside the room, it's hard to tell what time it is. It's even hard to tell that it's summer.

The Man locks the door behind him and moves to stand by the corner of the bed. He takes off his shoes, his glasses, each sock, and then he starts to unbutton his shirt. Sweetheart watches him. He thinks he should get undressed too. He takes off his tank top. He throws his cut-offs down and they land wherever. Sweetheart sits down on the bed. The Man folds his pants in half and hangs them off the edge of the dresser. He sits next to Sweetheart. They look at each other, both in their underwear, unsure of where to start. The Man touches Sweetheart's cheek with the back of his palm. Then he takes his hand and slips it underneath the elastic waistband of Sweetheart's boxers.

†

After Miranda quit, the manager at the video store went even more batshit crazy. He cut everyone's hours while simultaneously making everyone stay late after their shifts without overtime. During this period, Sweetheart's overdue bills finally caught up to him. The phone company threatened to cut off service if he didn't pay in full by the end of the month. Ditto the internet. He owed his roommate money for rent from the month before and the month before that. Sweetheart knew he had to start looking for another job, but he was too tired after work, and on his days off he sat paralyzed with anxiety thinking about the bills. There just wasn't enough money.

August dragged on slow and heavy. Sweetheart ate bowls of rice fried in garlic, or nothing at all. Part of the reason he didn't look for another job was that somewhere inside him Sweetheart believed that if he just waited it out at the video store, things would get better. His manager would eventually have to adjust the schedule to suit the needs of his employees or else everyone would just quit and store would shut down. Miranda told him to stop being so unrealistic.

Then, a few days ago, The Man came into the video store for his weekly renewal.

"What's wrong?" said The Man when he came up to the cash. "You don't look so good." Sweetheart shrugged.

"Rent's due," he said.

"You don't make enough working here?" The Man asked.

"Barely," Sweetheart said. He felt his face get hot. He didn't want to cry, not here, not at work in front of some old man renting the same garbage porno for the millionth time. The Man leaned over the cash and touched Sweetheart's cheek with the back of his palm.

"Here," said The Man. "Take my number. Maybe I can help."

†

As he slowly pushes himself inside The Man, Sweetheart remembers a game he used to play at summer day camp as a child. The game is called "Darling, If You Love Me, Won't You Please, Please Smile?" The game goes like this: The person who is "it" stands in the centre of the circle. That person approaches someone in the circle and says, "Darling, if you love me, won't you please, please smile?" If the person in the centre of the circle can't convince you to smile by asking that question, they must move on and try to convince someone else. If you smile when asked to by the person in the centre of the circle, you replace them as "it." Sweetheart was never very good at this game. He doesn't know why he would always smile when the person in the centre of the circle would ask him to, even when they asked him in a goofy voice that he didn't find very funny. He just couldn't help it. This is what Sweetheart thinks about as he pushes himself into the body of The Man, who whispers, "I love your big black cock," into Sweetheart's ear, soft like the refrain of a lullaby.

†

After they finish, Sweetheart takes a shower. He feels reckless and dumb, but also invincible, like he just egged a house or smashed a car window. He catches falling water in his mouth and then spits it back out.

When Sweetheart comes out of the shower The Man is dressed again, doing up the final buttons on his shirt. Sweetheart picks his underwear off the floor and puts them on. He finds his tank top and cut-offs and puts them back on too. He sits on the edge of the bed to put on his socks. The Man is standing by the door smoking a cigarette.

"Do you want one?" he asks. He hands Sweetheart a pack of cigarettes and a lighter; tries to be smooth about it but fumbles and drops the lighter. Sweetheart picks it up from the floor, lights a cigarette, and looks down at his feet. There is grey carpeting, and above the two men, a ceiling fan that whirs. Sweetheart feels almost bad for him, The Man with The Kids and The Job, who stares at the motel door like it's a window leading to someplace else.

"So how much do I owe you?" The Man asks. Sweetheart doesn't know.

"Two hundred bucks?" he says.

"I'll give you a hundred," says The Man. "Because I brought the condoms and that's supposed to be your job."

A hundred bucks isn't enough to cover the missing part of the rent. Sweetheart doesn't know how to fight it. He smiles.

"A hundred is fine," he says. If he does this again, he'll remember to bring his own condoms.

†

Back in the grey minivan, Sweetheart has the peculiar feeling of moving in reverse while hurtling forward. Here it is again, the nowhere space, not inside the city but not outside of it either. A patch of grass. A billboard ad. The tall buildings of downtown just at the tip of the vanishing point.

Inside the grey minivan it is silent. The Man prefers it

that way. Sweetheart texts Miranda, who tells him to get his ass to the beach. It is summer, after all. And still early. Plenty of daylight left to spare.

The Man pulls into the passenger pickup area of the subway station at the end of the line. He stops the car in front of the subway entrance. He turns to face Sweetheart.

"I'll see you around," he says.

"Yeah, sure," says Sweetheart, smiling, uncertain if either one of them means it.

"Well, then," says The Man. "'Til next time."

Sweetheart nods. He climbs out of the grey minivan, slams the door, and watches it drive away. It gets smaller and smaller until it is someplace else.

Sweetheart sticks his hand into the pocket of his cutoffs and rubs the crisp one-hundred dollar bill between his fingers. Tomorrow he has a shift at the video store. The day after that, rent is due. Today he will go to the beach.

# THE COMING ATTRACTIONS

GOING TO the movies stoned is totally this thing. You usually go to those superhero movies, the ones that become these big multi-picture franchises. It used to be trendy for superhero movies to be campy like in the '90s, but now they're always in 3D and each one is described as darker than the last. They have these big budgets and they're all basically the same, and look, there's the president, white skin and white balding hair, a suit and tie, some actor you've never heard of 50 times your size. You know these movies aren't any good but they're a fun way to pass the high.

Tonight is just the same. Your one friend, the one who organizes, sends out a mass Facebook message and then you and all your friends meet half an hour before the movie starts to smoke a joint in the little park on Metcalfe down the street from the Scotiabank Theatre at Peel metro. You cram six to a bench in a long, straight row. Everyone gets giggly and then silent. A homeless man asks you for a cigarette.

†

You walk into the theatre and you're buzzing from the weed, so stoned and obvious. The lights in the atrium are bright and it feels like there are a lot of people around, standing in line to buy their tickets. The sparkly grey-purple vinyl that coats the floors is covered in a layer of brown slush. It's a Montreal winter. There's snow fucking everywhere, even indoors. To your right hangs a wall of framed posters, each one advertising one of the movies currently playing at the theatre.

You're like, "Why do movie posters always look like that? They always look kind of the same, y'know what I mean?"

Your friends are like, *What the fuck are you talking about?* Everyone lines up and sheepishly buys their ticket. You think you have enough money for the movie. You checked your bank balance this morning and there was enough, just barely, but you bought cheap beer and a pack of cigarettes, which probably set you back 10 or 15 bucks. Your credit's maxed out. You'll have to find a way to make it work 'til payday next week. Plus, you have to get popcorn. The best part of going to the movies is the popcorn. You know that it's basically nothing but salt and butter, but that's why you like it—you can keep eating more and more and you'll never get full. It's like paying a lot of money to eat air.

When it's your turn to buy your ticket you pay on debit. You never carry cash. You try not to show your relief when the transaction is approved. You pull your debit card out of the terminal and put it back in your wallet, taking the ticket from the cashier like it's no big deal, like of course your card wouldn't get declined. Next to you, your friend laughs.

She's like, "I totally forgot how to use the debit machine."

You're like, "Haha, yeah." You look down at the ticket, the paper waxy and weightless between your fingers. It costs $12.99 to see a movie.

†

The escalator is steep, like the ascent of a roller coaster. It is only anticipation. You go up and up and up but never down. Kids whip past, racing. They're sneaking into R-rated movies, going on their first dates. You crack a beer concealed in a plastic bag. One of the kids, maybe 13 and a little overweight, slower than the others, gives you a conspiratorial smile. Everyone is being bad tonight.

You think about the darkness of the theatre, public and concealed, a party where you can't see any of the guests. You once had a lover who only wanted to meet you in the backs of movie theatres. This was a few years ago now. You met online. You were 18. He was older and "discreet," didn't host. You didn't want to host him in case your roommates thought it was sketchy to invite some random 40-year-old over for sex. He suggested Cinéma L'Amour on St. Laurent. You had never been anywhere like that before, and when he suggested it, you were skeptical/nervous but also curious/thrilled, so of course you agreed. You met on the corner and went into the theatre together without saying a word, you 10 paces behind him. You thought it was sexy: the sticky floors, his hand groping for your crotch in the blackness, feeling yourself get hard from that unseen touch, the moaning of porn stars surrounding but distant. You met him there many times, your very own undercover lover. You met him in similar theatres too, one in the Village and another on St. Hubert. He never wanted to see you in the light, and as much as that hurt you, you didn't want to see him in the light either. He was always so paranoid that someone might see you together. He'd make you come 15 minutes after him and search for his face among the rows of seats, forcing your eyes to adjust to the dark. He had a tattoo of a red swallow just under his left eye, which is what you would look for to find him.

Eventually the secrecy of the encounters lost their appeal. The whole coming-fifteen-minutes-later/staying-ten-paces-behind thing became so tedious and annoying that it was no longer fun and you stopped replying to his texts. He was upset and would send you long, angry messages in the middle of the night. You felt bad, but not that bad. *Whatever,* you think. *He probably has some other boy by now.*

There's an usher at the top of the escalator. You hand them your ticket and they rip it in two, hand the divided halves back to you. They mumble something about theatre six or maybe it's seven, at the end of the hall to the left. You never listen to what the ushers tell you. They don't really care if you listen. They're just spitting out the phrases their bosses told them to say so they won't get fired. "Enjoy the show," they say. Like a suggestion, a piece of advice halfheartedly delivered and not expected to be taken: You might like it better if you try to enjoy it.

†

Everyone needs to pee so the group fans out to the bathrooms, boys to the left and girls to the right. You hate the men's room. The macho bravado of the whole thing makes you anxious. The man with the swallow tattoo first suggested that you meet in a public washroom, but you said no. To suck dick in a men's room stall felt pretty badass in this *fuck you* kind of way, but you were too afraid of what could happen if you got caught, especially if police got involved. Now you sort of wish that you had just said yes.

It's just you and one other guy from the group in the bathroom. You know him, but not too well. He's your friend's boyfriend who gets dragged around to things like this. He always looks slightly bored and doesn't talk all that much, resigned to the fact that that's what good boyfriends do. There is one urinal of space in between you.

The boyfriend looks at you, briefly, but it's only to check that you aren't looking at him. When you're hanging out in a group he always engages you in conversation or tries to instil some sense of camaraderie, at least for his girlfriend's sake, but when you're alone he becomes uncomfortable. You make him nervous. Sometimes, you catch his slight recoil before he puts something nicer in front of it. If one of his buddies says something when you're around, he'll look to you and then to his girlfriend, and then he'll go, *C'mon, man, be cool,* to his friend all serious, like he's defending your honour, but he'll say it with his head down, soft enough to be a whisper, like he doesn't know what he's saying or why. Later, when you're alone with his girlfriend, your friend, she'll be like, *See? Isn't he a good guy?* And you'll nod, silent. You will never know what he says to his friends, alone without their girlfriends, drinking beer in the back of the bar or whatever. You will never truly know him.

You look at yourself in the mirror as you wash your hands. You feel so ugly. Need a shave. You know you're still so young because that's what everyone tells you, but you're starting to notice a bitterness in your eyes that wasn't always there. You sense yourself becoming hardened against the world in a way that feels disappointing yet inevitable. Before you met, the man with the swallow tattoo asked you to send him a picture of your face. After you sent it to him, he said you were the most beautiful boy he had ever seen and you were prepared to believe him, even though in retrospect it sounds like such an obvious line. You splash some water on your face and watch it drip down your brown cheeks. You leave the washroom without drying your hands because whatever, fuck it, who cares?

Outside the washroom, you and your friend, the one who couldn't remember how to work the debit machine, wait for everyone to finish up. You hand her the beer you've been nursing, still wrapped in the plastic bag. She takes a sip.

She's like, "He's so random, who even invited him? She should just break up with him already, she could do way better." You laugh.

"I know, right? If I have to sit next to him during the movie I'll totally kill myself."

"Oh my God, shoot me." She takes another swig and hands the can back to you. The boyfriend comes out of the bathroom.

"Hey, can I have a sip?" he asks.

You're like, "Sorry, it's done," and you take one last big gulp for dramatic effect. You throw the can in the trash and you and your friend turn and walk away. You're both giggling. She grabs your arm, making a big show of being inconspicuous. You're still stoned and being a bitch, and it is so much fun.

† 

You get in line at the concession stand. A large rectangular box made of glass sits in the centre behind the cash, the heart of the whole operation, circulating popcorn like blood. Your other friends join you in line. You ask each other, "What are you going to get, what are you going to get?" You look at the menu, mounted overhead on a flat, glowing screen. The combos each have a little picture and their prices are really, really big. The prices of the items individually are really, really small; almost hidden. The medium is about four times the size of the small. It would be stupid not to give them 75 more cents. It's your bright idea, not theirs. They just told it to you. They're trying to give you a deal. Your friend and her boyfriend are behind you in line, his arm around her shoulders. They're going to share popcorn, the way that lovers do. You wonder when they're going to break up.

You haven't thought about the man with the face tattoo in a long time, but he was sort of in this dream you had the other night. In the dream you could see the whole city from way up high, but you weren't flying. It wasn't one of those dreams. You were the sky. From that vantage point you could see that Montreal was an island. You always knew it was, but you never really took it in. You could see St. Laurent Boulevard as a thin straight line, from Chinatown all the way up to Chabanel and then beyond, to parts of the city you've never explored. You saw your old apartment in St. Henri, the vegan restaurant where you wash dishes, your current apartment on the western edge of the Plateau, that dep you like. You saw groups of friends hanging out, in living rooms in the winter and rooftops in the summer, at vernissages and house shows. You were everywhere, the centre of everything and yet totally diffuse. It was the city as you knew it but also another place entirely, the people both familiar and strange, the buildings pink and blue and puffy like marshmallows.

You saw men. So many men. In parks and bathrooms and alleyways, behind the graveyard on top of the mountain. You saw a movie theatre full of men. Rows and rows of them, watching a movie that was all fuzzy and without audio, like there was something wrong with the projector. It's common knowledge that men from Montreal make the best lovers, bad teeth and bad jobs, but they sure knew how to please a boy and now you were one of them, in the plush seats of the movie theatre eating your popcorn. You were the sky and a red swallow flew through you. You didn't want the dream to end, but you knew that it would and it did.

† 

There's only one person ahead of you in line, giving their

order to the concession stand cashier. You can't afford the popcorn. If you buy it, you'll have less than 20 bucks to last you the week. But you're already in line and you want it so bad, because what's a movie without popcorn? Who would be willing to lend you some money? Who haven't you asked recently? Who do you not already owe? You watch one of the employees stir melted butter in a vat with a big metal spoon, like a grandmother hunched over an old family recipe. What's the deal with those payday loans places? Maybe you could go to one of those. Another employee takes a big metal scoop and doles popcorn into an oversized and colourful paper bag. You watch the kernels bounce and float in their large glass tank, like dandelion fluff blown from its stem.

You want a bag of bottomless popcorn. You want to have the next handful ready in your fist before you've even finished chewing. You want so much popcorn that your sweat will turn to butter, the same buttery sweat as when he touched you in the back of that theatre when you were just a sexy young thing like everybody wants to be. You want to be full of it, this thing that can never make you full. When did you become this insatiable? Somebody taps you on the shoulder from behind. A cashier is waiting to serve you.

# OUR LADY OF PERPETUAL REALNESS

BRONSON INVITES everyone to a drag BBQ on a Saturday night. Mada and Kalale are not really that down but they'll go. Paul wants us all to have amazing looks. I'm excited but try not to show it. I go shopping at Renaissance and the woman who works at the changing rooms looks at me funny when I keep bringing dresses and skirts to try on. I try on a skirt and it looks great with the white button-down I'm wearing, so I decide to do a Catholic schoolgirl look. I grab a tie that matches the skirt. I have dangling cross earrings that'll be perfect.

†

At the BBQ there are chips and meat and plenty of beer. There are wigs and dresses and Paul has a killer pair of heels but the energy is a little low. Everyone is feeling tired. We're hungover from partying yesterday, or we're in school or we've been working hard all week, in restaurants and bars, in retail and low-level office jobs.

Paul brings me a blonde wig that I tie back into a ponytail to show off the earrings. Meredith does my makeup: pink lips and smudged eyeliner.

"It looks so good," my friends say. "It's so messy. Like you just gave the quarterback a blowjob."

Nobody can agree on where to go out. Bronson's original plan was to go to the Village, but not everyone is down. There's a rave at the train tracks and Cousins at Le Ritz and an after-hours at the Durocher lofts. Drugs arrive and make everything more confusing.

Tony told her friends to meet us in the Village, but everyone keeps flip-flopping. The boys decide to go to Sky Bar. Mada is meeting up with Lindsey at the train tracks. Kalale is like, *Fuck no, I'm not going to the village.* The crew splits up. I tell Kalale I want to show off my look. She's like, *Yeah, with the boys.* She's right. I know what she means when she says it.

†

In the Uber, my wig is hot and my makeup is smearing. Joel is already at Sky Bar, on the rooftop patio. This makes us all very excited. I crack the window, stick my head out for the breeze.

"I tend to go rogue in Village bars," I say.

"Please don't," says Paul. "We have to stick together."

†

Outside Sky Bar we smoke a cigarette, take a few snaps,

try to hype each other up. Everyone on St. Catherine is just in their civilian drag. We definitely stand out. Nobody shaved their facial hair, so pieces of wig keep getting caught in our beards. For Paul there are sandals inside my backpack, in case he gets tired in heels. I sling it over one shoulder like a delinquent Catholic school girl in the movies.

"You look like the bitchiest girl from my high school," says Leah. "Her name was Laura Michelle." Leah is wearing a pristine grey wig and long chiffon robe. She looks incredible, like an eccentric yet refined art professor.

"OMG totally," I say. "I'm totally Laura Michelle right now."

†

The bar is multi-levelled so for a while we scamper from floor to floor, trying to find our bearings. We perform for each other, as if to be like, *Yeah cool c'mon let's go!* We have to keep each other confident. There are hundreds of people in the bar, but it's spread out so that every new room looks somehow under-filled.

A bouncer shows us up to the rooftop patio. We meet Joel at a table and order drinks. Things get quiet. The energy is calmer up here. There's a breeze. You can see the tops of buildings, but nothing's tall enough to obstruct the dark blue sky.

I wish the others were here to laugh and throw shade. I text Mada and tell her that I love her.

We go back into the club and dance a little bit more.

People come up to Paul and compliment him on his look. People come up to Bronson and people come up to Joel. Nobody comes up to me except the bouncer, who says I have to check my bag and then escorts me by the arm to the coat check. All the people I came here with are white. I don't have any change for the coat check so I try to get them to check my bag for free, but they're not having it so I stash it in the corner. This is the only time I go rogue at Sky Bar.

†

Back at Bronson's, everyone is feeling tired again. It's around 3 a.m. and we're running low on cigarettes. We decide that if we're going to make it to the after-hours we have to leave soon, otherwise we'll lose steam. We drink the last of the beers and sprinkle the rest of the drugs into cups of water that we knock back quickly. Bronson and Joel take off their wigs. They're equally handsome, with or without them. I take my wig off too. Mada texts me and says that she loves me.

"So you're not going to wear your drag anymore?" asks Paul. Nobody answers. He's upset. "I don't want to be the only one in drag. You only want to take it off so you can get laid."

He has a point. I do want to get laid and I do think that this will be easier to accomplish out of drag. I do potentially want to go rogue at the after-hours and I think that will be easier to accomplish out of drag as well. I feel gross for thinking these things.

But it's more complicated than that. This is only

a week after the mass shooting at Pulse Nightclub in Orlando. Forty-nine people died. This is after years of violent attacks against trans women and black men.

It's why we're all so tired, at least in part. It creates an extra layer of fatigue: Where do we go to dance fucked up all night long and not die? Where do we go to get laid and not die? Who is here in this room with us? Who is not here in this room with us? What are we going to wear? Who will get harassed on the street, by the police or a random stranger or someone we all know, sometimes in darkness but often in broad daylight, in the exact same look that any of us could've been wearing? How are we going to get home?

†

Paul catches a cab outside of Bronson's and ushers the group inside it. We're all in our drag again. He's convinced us. I wish I could explain how beautiful Paul looks tonight, in the $300 blue sequin dress and the suede pumps pinching his toes.

"C'mon, get in," he says to me.

"No," I say. "That's alright. You guys go on without me. I think I'm just gonna walk home."

Paul gives me an irritated look, but he's past the point of caring enough to convince me to go out. It's too late. He gets in the cab and slams the door. He just wants to party. The cab drives away. I've gone rogue.

†

I stop at a 24-hour gas station to buy cigarettes. I look at myself in the screen of the security camera. My wig is missing. It must've fallen off somewhere on the street, or maybe I wasn't actually wearing it when I left Bronson's. I can't remember. The eyeliner's smudgy. My lips are a big pink smear. Meredith touched them up before we left.

It's 4 a.m. and the sun is rising on St. Laurent. On the street I walk slowly and deliberately, heel-toe, heel-toe. The street is empty. No one is there to brush past me. All the businesses are closed. I walk past the roti shop, the interior design place, the sports bar that used to be a gay bar two years ago, when I got a public urination ticket for peeing in the alley outside of it.

When do you have the opportunity to just completely feel yourself like this? I turn the street into my runway. I hold my arms open, palms up, my backpack slung over one shoulder. My earrings, they dangle. The swish of my skirt. My head is held to the sky that turns baby blue and pink with morning. It's sticky and hot. So hot. I can feel the makeup dripping down my face. My feet hurt but I own it. Heel-toe, heel-toe, heel-toe. I'm almost home. There's an electro beat that thumps to the west. Through the chirps of the birds I can hear it.

## NOTES

"California Underwater" first appeared in *Bad Nudes*. "Darling, If You Love Me" first appeared in *Matrix Magazine*. "Our Lady of Perpetual Realness" first appeared in *Cosmonauts Avenue*.

# ACKNOWLEDGEMENTS

Thank you to all the friends, peers, and editors who took the time to look over earlier drafts of these stories. Thank you to Jay Ritchie and Ashley Opheim for the continued support and mentorship and for the kick in the butt I needed to put this collection together. Thank you to Fraser Wrighte for being totally in sync with me and creating a beautiful cover. Thank you to Madelyne, Kalale, and Delilah for absolutely everything. Thank you to my family. Thank you to Zoe, for getting it more than anyone.

Cason Sharpe is a writer born and raised in Toronto and currently living in Montreal. He has a BA from Concordia University in Political Science, Creative Writing, and Sexuality Studies. He is the recipient of The Renée Vautelet Prize for Political Science. He is the web coordinator for *carte blanche* and one half of the podcast *TwoHungryChildren*.